D0607140

Fountain of Fire

written and illustrated by

Gill McBarnet

Ruwanga Trading

Also published by Rawanga Trading Inc:
The Whale Who Wanted to be Small
The Wonderful Journey
The Pink Parrot
A Whale's Tale
The Shark who Learned a Lesson
The Goodnight Gecko
Gecko Hide And Seek

First published 1987 by
Rawanga Trading Inc.
P.O. Box 1027
Puunene
Hawaii 96784

Printed and bound in Hong Kong
under direction of:
Mandarin Offset

ISBN 0-9615102-3-4

© 1987 Gill McBarnet

For Monica

It was like any other day in Hawaii when Lani came home from school. Her mother waved from the house, and Koa barked and ran to meet her. Her pet Nene goose was also happy to see her. A few weeks ago Lani found him in the forest, wounded and starving. Now he followed her about the house — limping because he was not yet strong enough to fly.

The sun shone in a bright blue sky and a soft breeze cooled her cheeks. It seemed like any other day.

But something was different.

The animals in the forest sensed danger. The wild pigs trotted this way and that. The mongoose scurried about, quick and alert. In the tree high above, the owl looked worried.

Even the small birds were restless.

Bright as jewels, they flew twittering from tree to tree.

Suddenly, the house began to shake.

"An earth tremor!" her mother said. The windows
rattled, the cups clattered and the picture swung about on the wall.
Lani comforted her goose. He was frightened and flapped his wings.
She smoothed his feathers and took him in her arms.

Then the shaking stopped . . . as suddenly as it had started.

That night the volcano erupted. Like a fountain of fire, it exploded rock and red hot lava into the darkening sky. It looked angry, and Lani was frightened.

"Don't be afraid," said her father. "I've seen the volcano erupt many times. The fountain of fire is too far away to hurt us, but the lava spilling down the side of the volcano is like a river of fire flowing slowly down to the sea, burning everything in its path. It is not coming in our direction, but if it does we will have to leave our house."

The next day the lava flow **did** change direction. It was now moving towards the village.

Lani's Grandma and Grandpa lived outside the village, near the lava flow. Lani and her father went to help them. The lava was coming towards the house! Lani could smell the trees burning. It was getting closer and closer. She helped Grandma pack the truck.

The men tried to put out the flames — but it was no use. The jet of water hissed and turned to steam.

"We must go!" Lani's father shouted. As they drove quickly away, Lani looked back and this is what she saw.

All that remained of Grandma and Grandpa's house was the red tin roof. The lava smashed and burnt the house and every tree that stood in its way. Lani knew that it would soon destroy the old mango tree she loved to climb, and the bike that they had not had time to throw into the back of the truck. . .

All the people of the village went to church.

Outside the church, Lani touched the cool black rock of a lava flow of long long ago. The lava spilling down the volcano today was fiercely hot, and Lani wondered if their house and the little white church would also be destroyed — like Grandma and Grandpa's house.

That night the sky was a dark orange, and the fountain of fire looked angrier than *ever* before. The lava kept moving slowly towards the village.

"We'll be safe tonight, but tomorrow we must leave our house," said Lani's father.
Lani's mother said, "I'm sad we have to leave our lovely house." Lani also felt sad. She hoped with all her heart that their house would not be destroyed.

Early the next morning, they packed the truck and were ready to go.

"Come along!" Lani's father suddenly shouted. "The lava is flowing down a steep hill. It's moving quickly. We must go." As they sped away, Lani turned and looked at the house. Something moved. It was her goose! In the confusion of packing up, they had forgotten the goose, and there he was — limping after them.

"Stop!" Lani shouted, but her father did not hear her above the roar of the engine. There was no time to spare. She had to jump out and save her goose.

Lani ran as fast as she could. She could see the lava as it moved closer and closer. She could smell the burning and feel the heat of the lava as it moved towards the house. She scooped up the goose and looked wildly around to see which way she should run.

The lava was almost upon her. Suddenly she felt alone and very frightened. What should she do? Where could she run?

Just in time, her father raced up to her. He had seen her run back to the house, and now he had come back to save her. He lifted her into his arms and carried her to the top of the hill next to their house.

"High ground is our only hope" he said. They huddled together . . . and then the most amazing thing happened. When the lava reached the bottom of the hill, it started to flow **around** the hill. Away from the house, away from the hill and away from the rest of the village!

The people of the village were very happy.

They were safe now: the river of fire had turned away from their homes, their shops and the school. It had even spared the little white church, and now they all gathered to watch the lava disappear into the sea with an angry HISS!

The fountain of fire gradually disappeared.

Grandma and Grandpa started to build a new house on the hill next to Lani's house. Grandpa told everyone he thought it was the safest place in Hawaii!

"We are beginning all over again," he told Lani one day. "Just like this little fern which is beginning a new life. It is growing out of the lava flow that has cooled and hardened into black rock. Hot lava destroys . . . but it cools and in time it becomes home for many different plants and animals."

Lani's goose is also beginning all over again. Now that his wing has healed, he can fly back to where the wild geese live on the volcano high above the village. He will miss Lani and will always remember her kindness, but the volcano is his home.

Happy and free, he flies up and up towards the silent volcano.